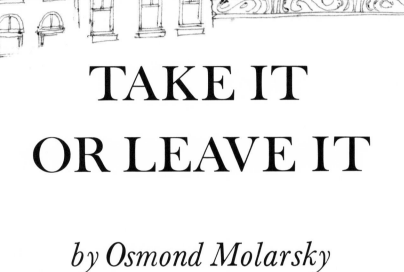

# TAKE IT
# OR LEAVE IT

*by Osmond Molarsky*

*illustrated by Trina Schart Hyman*

*Henry Z. Walck, Inc.*      *New York*

Molarsky, Osmond
  Take it or leave it; illus. by
Trina Schart Hyman.   Walck, 1971
  64p.  illus.

  Chester was a champion swapper,
until the day he found he needed the
worst end of the trade to get what he
really wanted.


1. Swapping - Fiction  2. Urban life -
Fiction  I. Illus.  II. Title

*This Main Entry catalog card may be reproduced without permission.*

*For Peggy*

"I'll swap you," Chester said.

Who did he say it to? It didn't matter. He said it to anybody who had something he wanted. And Chester always wanted what somebody else had.

One day Chester was standing in front of Firehouse No. 23, playing with his Yo-Yo. Along came Walter, minding his own business, counting his baseball cards. "Forty-six," Walter was saying, as he came up to Chester.

"I'll swap you," Chester said.

"Huh?" Walter said, looking up.

"I'll swap you my Yo-Yo for your baseball cards," Chester said, flicking out the Yo-Yo and making it snap back into his hand smartly.

"I don't want to swap," Walter said. "I've got almost a full set, only four more to go."

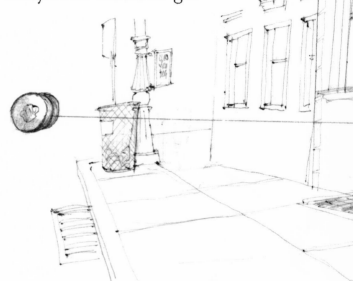

"It's up to you," Chester said, flinging the Yo-Yo out almost under Walter's nose and making him flinch. "I swapped an Official Boy Scout knife for this Yo-Yo. It's made of real boxwood."

"Real boxwood? What's that?"

"It's what they make the best Yo-Yos out

of," Chester said. "Take it or leave it." And he
zoomed the Yo-Yo and zapped a soda bottle
right off a ledge.

"I'll take it," Walter said. Watching the Yo-
Yo had made Walter woozy. Quick as a flash, the
cards and the Yo-Yo changed hands. Chester
had the cards, and Walter had the Yo-Yo.

"So long," Chester said, fanning out the
cards and starting down the street, as Walter
slipped the Yo-Yo cord over his finger and
began to practice with it.

Chester had not gone very far when he met Pendleton, coming from the other direction, on his skate scooter.

"Where'd you get the skate scooter?" Chester asked.

"Made it," said Pendleton.

"Thought maybe you swapped something for it," Chester said.

"Nope," Pendleton said.

"Got almost a full set of baseball cards," Chester said.

"How many you got to go?"

"Only four."

"That's pretty good," said Pendleton.

"Want to swap?" said Chester.

"Swap what?"

"Your skate scooter for my baseball cards."

"Nah—this is a neat scooter."

"These are neat cards," Chester said, and he fanned them out and also riffled them, with a

riffling noise. Pendleton's eyes bugged out, as he watched Chester do things with the cards. He was getting confused.

"I dunno," said Pendleton, admiring the skate scooter that he had built, himself.

"Take it or leave it," said Chester, taking a step, as if to walk away.

"I'll take it," Pendleton said, and before he knew it he was holding the cards and watching Chester speed off on his skate scooter.

Chester covered quite a few blocks of the city on his new homemade skate scooter, and he did it in a very short time. Luckily for him there were no speed limits for skate scooters and there were no laws against no-hand driving, sitting-down, hand-standing or backward coasting on hills. Luckily, too, he knocked nobody down. He certainly gave more than one lady a terrible fright, as he wove in and out among the people on the sidewalk, at the speed of zap.

As Chester rolled up to the corner of Seventh and Oak, he slowed down long enough to see Murdock walking toward the park with a boomerang. "Hey, Murdock—want to swap?"

"No," said Murdock, who had known Chester for a long time. "I'm not going to swap my brand new boomerang for an old homemade skate scooter. You can save your breath."

"That's up to you," said Chester, weaving up the sidewalk, making a sharp U turn and weaving back. "This skate scooter may be homemade, but the skates are brand new, the foot board is one-inch plywood, and the engine hood is a box that fresh rutabagas came in." Chester wasn't sure that rutabagas had come in the box, but he wasn't sure that they hadn't, either.

"What are rutabagas?" said Murdock.

"They're something like...well, artichokes, only bigger," said Chester. He wasn't sure they were like artichokes, but how could he be sure they weren't?

"What are artichokes?" said Murdock.

"You're changing the subject."

"What subject?"

"You know what subject. Either you want the skate scooter or you don't want it. Take it or leave it." Chester waited a second, then

started to scoot away, except that he made another sharp U turn and ended up exactly where he had started, in front of Murdock.

"I never saw a skate scooter make a U turn like that," Murdock said.

"And you never will again," Chester said.

"I'll take it," said Murdock, handing over his brand new boomerang and hopping on the scooter and scooting away. For just one moment, Chester thought maybe he had made a bad swap. Well, he would see how well the boomerang worked, before he decided.

A block or two along, he came to the park. Finding a wide-open space, without too many trees around, he let fly with the boomerang, side-arm.

Away it went, far, wide and high, then back it wheeled and dropped at Chester's feet. Neat, thought Chester. A neat boomerang, and he threw it again. A lucky swap, he thought. He was pleased with the boomerang and with himself.

Chester practiced with the boomerang until he could make it sail out and clip leaves off the branch of a big tree at the far side of the clearing, then sail back and drop at his feet, as if a dog had fetched it. Chester had just thrown the boomerang for the fifteenth time when suddenly he noticed a boy watching him. The boy was leaning on the strangest contraption Chester had ever seen—a bicycle with only one wheel and no handlebars. "What's that?" Chester asked.

"A monocycle," the boy said. "My father couldn't afford to buy me the other wheel. Ha, ha, ha!"

Chester could tell it was a joke the boy told every time he had the chance, so he didn't laugh. "How do you ride it?" he asked.

The boy got on the seat, put his feet on the pedals and started to ride around and around in circles. Chester remembered then that he had seen a bear ride one in a circus. If a bear could learn to do it, so could he, thought Chester. "I'll swap you for this boomerang," he said.

"My pop would be mad, if I swapped my monobike," the boy said.

"Your pop would be mad if you missed a chance to get this great boomerang for nothing but a measly one-wheel bike."

"Let me try it out and see if I like it," the boy said.

"All right," Chester said. "I'll hold your wheel."

The boy, who happened to be a good pitcher, hurled the boomerang far out across the clearing. He watched it sail far, far out, then curve gracefully around and drop right at his feet. "Neat," he said. "I'll swap you."

Chester was taken by surprise. He hadn't even had time to say, "Take it or leave it," before the boy had decided. It was almost too easy. But Chester knew a good swap when he saw one, so he said, "I'll take it."

Learning to ride the wheel was not so easy. It was twice as hard as riding a two-wheel bike. For one thing, there were no handlebars, only pedals, so "no hands" was the only way he could ride. It was half an hour before he could ride three feet in any direction without falling on his face or the seat of his pants.

But all in good time, Chester learned to ride the one-wheeler. He could ride it forward, and backward, and he could ride it around in backward and forward circles. The only thing he could not do was ride with his feet on the handlebars. So, full of daring, out of the park he pedaled and down Tilden Avenue, arms folded on his chest, thinking that maybe if he had a bear suit, he could get a job in a circus. Kind of hot, though, inside a bear suit, Chester thought to himself.

Just as he was deciding not to join a circus, he came to the Civic Center Plaza, where people were sitting about on the grass with their sandals off, and the pigeons were watching the sea gulls paddle in the Reflecting Pool. There at the pool, also, were some boys and a girl watching something in the water. Chester saw it was a perfect model nuclear submarine, diving, cruising under water, surfacing, then diving and cruising again. Up and down the pool it cruised, leaving a trail of bubbles wherever it went, and all the girl who owned it had to do was turn it around when it came to the end of the pool.

"What makes it go?" asked Chester.

"Power capsules," said the girl. "You put one in and wet it, and the sub goes for up to half an hour."

"Sensational," Chester said and stood there, leaning against his monobike, fascinated by the model submarine. If there was anything he ever wanted in his life, it was that model sub that ran for up to half an hour on a power capsule. How could he make a swap, especially with a girl?

Chester began to pedal up and down, beside the Reflecting Pool. First on one side of the pool, then on the other. There was a sign that said *No Bicycle Riding*, but that didn't bother Chester. He wasn't riding a bicycle, a bicycle had two wheels. By this time, Chester had learned to turn around and face backwards without even getting off the seat. This was enough to attract a lot of notice, and it was not long before all the kids who were watching the model nuclear sub turned to watch Chester. Even the girl, whose name turned out to be Susan, turned from her submarine to watch Chester ride.

Now is the time to begin the swap, Chester thought, coming to a stop right in front of Susan.

"Show-off!" Susan said.

"You, too, can be a show-off," Chester said.

"How?" said Susan.

"By learning to ride a wheel."

"I haven't got one."

"That's the trouble," said Chester. "But I'll tell you what I'll do. I'll swap you my wheel for your submarine."

"It has no handlebars," Susan said.

"It doesn't need them."

"It has no headlight. It has no bell. It has no tool case."

"It doesn't need a tool case—it never breaks down," Chester said.

"It has no carrying rack," Susan complained.

"Take it or leave it," said Chester, getting on the wheel and starting to pedal away.

"I'll take it!" shouted Susan, and Chester circled around, pedaled back, hopped off, took the power capsules and dashed over to the Reflecting Pool just as the submarine came up to the edge, where he could grab it.

He watched it dive, cruise and surface, then

dive again, leaving a fine trail of bubbles wherever it went.

Once a sea gull thought it was a fish and
picked it up, and Chester thought he was going
to fly away with it. That would have been an
end of swapping for that day. But the sea gull
realized that it was made of plastic and dropped
it in disgust.

Chester thought he would never get tired of the submarine. He could imagine sailing it in the bathtub, at home, then coming back tomorrow and sailing it in the pool. Maybe he would never swap it.

Looking up from his atomic submarine, after its twenty-seventh cruise across the Reflecting Pool, Chester saw an astonishing sight. It was a boy bouncing along on a huge rubber ball. The ball had a kind of handle or pommel, to hang onto at the top of it, like a Western saddle, so he wouldn't fall off. And the boy was bouncing along like a kangaroo. Chester was about to send his sub on another cruise. Instead, he took it out of the water and hurried over to where the boy was riding. The boy finally bounced to a stop, and a number of people went over to look.

"What do you call it?" said a man.

"Old Paint," said the boy.

"I don't mean its name," the man said. "What is it?"

"It's a Kangaroo Bucking Ball," the boy said. "You can see it on television."

By this time, Chester had collected his wits. Walking up to the boy, he said, right out, "Want to swap?" He figured the best thing to do was come right to the point. He was holding the submarine behind him.

"For what?" the boy said.

Slowly Chester brought the submarine out in front of him. "For this capsule-powered

nuclear submarine that dives, cruises and sur-
faces for up to half an hour on one power
capsule. Advertised on the Captain Stardust
show. It's sensational. Come on. I'll show you
how it works.''

Bouncing along on his Kangaroo Bucking
Ball, the boy followed Chester to the Reflecting
Pool. Chester put a fresh power capsule in the

sub and released it in the pool. It performed perfectly, and Chester could see that he might very well have a deal, for the boy's eyes kept getting bigger and bigger, as the sub dived and cruised and surfaced and dived again.

"Pretty good," said the boy, getting off the ball.

"What can you do with a ball like that in the bathtub?" Chester asked.

"Not much," said the boy.

"That's just the point," said Chester. "What do you say?"

"I don't know," said the boy.

The sub was just approaching the side of the pool. Chester grabbed it. Now was the time. "Take it or leave it," he said and looked impatient, as if he were in a hurry to go home.

"Now, wait just a second," said the boy.

"I've got to go," said Chester.

"I'll take it," said the boy.

One leap and Chester was astride the ball and bounding away down the Civic Center Plaza like a rodeo wrangler on a bronc. This was really great. Better than the skate scooter or the monobike. Better than the pogo stick he had once gotten in a swap. This was the best swapping Chester had ever done, and if he ever did any more, he would have to start with something else, not his Kangaroo Bucking Ball. This was something he would keep for his very own.

Chester had just made up his mind about this, when he saw a boy with a small black puppy on a string. The boy was jerking on the string and hitting the puppy with a stick. Chester bounded up to the boy and puppy. "Cut out hitting that puppy," Chester said.

"I'll hit it if I want to. It belongs to me," the boy said.

"It belongs to itself," said Chester. "Where did you get it?"

"I swapped a roller skate for it," the boy said.

Another swapper, thought Chester.

The puppy was all black, except for one white foot. His hair was silky, his ears were floppy at the ends, and his eyes were big, black and shining. He looked miserable and afraid of the boy who had him.

"What's his name?" asked Chester.

"I dunno," said the boy, yanking on the string and giving the puppy a whack on the back with the stick.

"If I had him, I'd call him Blackie," said Chester. He'd have given anything in the world, even the Kangaroo Bucking Ball, to have the puppy. But he knew he couldn't keep him, if he brought him home. He had tried twice before, and his mother wouldn't let him. She said they had no room to keep a dog, and it was true. But he had to get the puppy away from the boy. No telling how mean the boy might be to the puppy, if he got the chance.

"Ever ride on a Kangaroo Bucking Ball?" Chester said, bounding up and down in one place.

"No," said the boy.

"Want to try?" Chester knew it was easy and fun, right off.

"Okay," said the boy. "Here—hold my dog."

Chester took the string that held the dog. He threw the stick into the bushes. He kneeled down and petted the puppy, who was afraid of him at first, then waggled up to him and licked his hand.

Meanwhile, the boy straddled the ball, grabbed hold of the handle and bounded away

for a ride. He went so far that Chester thought he wasn't coming back, and that would have been fine. Chester would have just kept the dog and considered it a swap. But the boy came bouncing back, stopped in front of Chester and the pup, and got off.

Chester said, "Want to swap? I'll take your dog in trade."

"An old ball for a dog?" the boy said. "You think I'm crazy?"

"It's just a mutt," said Chester. "Probably six different breeds all in one."

"Then why do you want it?"

"I like mutts," said Chester.

"So do I," said the boy. "I won't swap."

He likes to be mean to mutts—that's what he means, thought Chester. Now, Chester was an old swapper, and very experienced. So he always kept something very special in reserve, for hard swaps. Just now it was a Japanese yen —a piece of brass money with a hole in the middle of it. He kept it in a special bag that hung on a string around his neck.

"Here's what I can do," Chester said, pulling the bag up out of his shirt front. "I can throw in a lucky Japanese coin. What do you say?"

The coin was not worth as much as an American penny, but being in the bag on a string around Chester's neck made it look very valuable. If he ever had to swap the yen, he would put something else in the bag to take its place, for another hard swap. Chester put the yen in the boy's hand and let him look at it. "Well?" he said.

The boy had a look in his eye, as if he might ask for still something else. "I dunno," he said, giving a hard jerk on the puppy's string.

"Take it or leave it," Chester said, and started to bounce away on the ball.

"Just a minute," the boy said, picking up another stick. Chester stopped. "What else will you throw into the swap?"

"Nothing," said Chester, and started to leave again.

"I'll take it," said the boy. "Here—take the mutt."

And that is how Chester got a dog that he
could not keep and would have to swap before
he went home for supper—or take to the dog
pound, and he didn't want to do that. "Come
on, Blackie," he said. "I've got to swap you
—to some kid who likes you and who can keep
you. I wish it was me."

In the next hour, Blackie trotted along at Chester's heels, while Chester tried to swap him for a baseball glove, for a bent hub cap, for a flashlight with a dead battery, for a kite with no string, for a roller skate and for four sticks of chewing gum. The trouble was that two of the boys didn't know if they could keep Blackie or not, and Chester was sure they couldn't. An-

other boy looked just as mean as the one who
had him in the first place. The one with the
hub cap didn't think a dog was worth a hub
cap, so Chester dropped the matter right there.
And when it came to swapping Blackie for four
sticks of gum, Chester just could not do it.
Maybe if it had been a whole pack. But a good
swapper like Chester! He just could not bring
himself to do it.

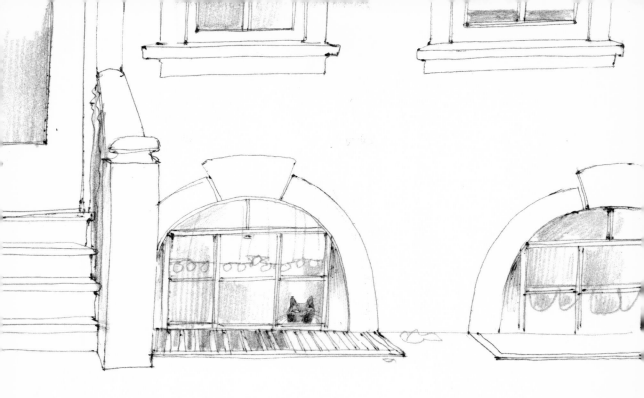

"After all, Blackie, I did swap a fantastic Kangaroo Bucking Ball for you," Chester said. "You wouldn't want me to give you away for four sticks of gum. Would you, now?"

By this time, Chester was back in his own neighborhood. How he wished he could take Blackie home with him. Maybe at least he could swap him with some kid who lived nearby. Then he could go see him once in a while.

Chester had not gotten very far past Fire-house No. 23 when who should he see but Walter, the boy who had swapped the baseball cards for the Yo-Yo. Walter was working the Yo-Yo, but not very well. It would come to the end of the string, roll up a little way, run down again and that would be about it. Walter just did not have a way with Yo-Yos.

"How're you doing with the Yo-Yo?" Chester asked.

"Not very great," said Walter. "I'd just as soon swap it back for the playing cards."

"Haven't got them," said Chester. "Swapped them for a skate scooter."

"Where's the skate scooter?" asked Walter.

"Haven't got it. Swapped it for a boomerang."

"Where's the boomerang?"

"Swapped it for a monobike."

"Where's the monobike?"

"Swapped it for a submarine powered with a power capsule."

"What did you swap the submarine for?"

"A Kangaroo Bucking Ball."

"A what?" said Walter. "What's that?"

"One of those things. They're neat. It doesn't matter. I swapped it for Blackie here."

"You sure did a lot of swapping today," said Walter.

"About average," said Chester.

"Are you through swapping for the day?" asked Walter. He was kneeling down by

Blackie, scratching him behind the ears, and Blackie was licking his hand.

"Why?" asked Chester.

"Would you swap Blackie for this Yo-Yo?" Walter asked.

"Will your mother let you have him?"

"Yup."

"How do you know?" said Chester.

"She said I could have a dog for my birthday," said Walter. "Tomorrow is my birthday. We were going to the pound tomorrow to pick one out. I pick Blackie, right now, if you want to swap."

Chester looked at the Yo-Yo. Looking at it one way, it wasn't a very good swap. A dog with as many breeds in him as Blackie was worth a dozen Yo-Yos. On the other hand, Blackie was worth nothing to Chester, because he couldn't keep him.

"Take it or leave it," said Walter.

"I'll take it," said Chester. He gave Blackie one last pat and handed him over. Walter gave him the Yo-Yo, and he put his finger through the loop in the cord. "Good-bye, Blackie," he said, then turned quickly and started toward his house, flicking the Yo-Yo out in all directions as he went. Tomorrow, he thought, would be another day.